ABDUCTED BY DARKNESS

AN ENEMIES-TO-LOVERS ROMANCE

LOXLEY CRESS

Paige,

Hope you have the best of holidays!

Loxley Cress

CONTENTS

CHAPTER 1

AVA

I was falling.

I had no idea how long I'd been falling or where I would land. Time lost all meaning, and the engulfing darkness stretched on endlessly. Desperation overtook me. I flailed my arms, attempting to grasp onto something, anything, but there was nothing but emptiness around me. My heart pounded in my chest, and panic threatened to consume me. I tried to scream, but no sound came out.

Just when I thought I might succumb to the fear, a strong arm encircled me, pulling me close to a solid chest. The presence of another person offered a glimmer of comfort in the abyss.

"Hold still," a low voice whispered in my ear, its warmth starkly contrasting with the cold void.

The weightlessness dissipated as abruptly as it had begun, and I found my feet on solid ground. Dizzy and unsteady, I attempted to step away from the person holding me, but my legs buckled in weakness. He caught me swiftly, cradling me in his arms as he carried me across a threshold.

The air here was different—crisp and cleaner. I felt a shift in the darkness surrounding us; it felt alive somehow. This was no longer the world I knew.

Where was I? What had happened to me?

My mind struggled to remember, but my memories were elusive, like fragments of a forgotten dream.

"Who are you?" I managed to murmur, my voice heavy with drowsiness and trepidation. "What did you do to me?"

The man holding me remained silent, his enigmatic presence adding to my confusion. He gently laid me on a bed.

"You're Malachi's problem now," he muttered, brushing away the strands of hair that clung to my face, his touch surprisingly tender.

Before I could ask any more questions, he turned away, walking toward the exit. At the door, he turned around hesitantly.

"Rest. You'll need it."

The sound of a lock clicking into place echoed in the silence, deepening my panic.

Kidnapped. I had been abducted.

My thoughts raced, trying to make sense of the situation. Who was this man, my captor? And who was Malachi?

I struggled to get out of bed, but dizziness overwhelmed me, pinning me back. A fragment of memory flashed across my mind.

Avaline. My name was Avaline, but everyone called me Ava.

I whispered my name to myself, clinging to the memory like a lifeline, hoping it would lead me back to my past. But that door remained stubbornly shut as if my memories had been intentionally veiled from me.

Frustration and fear gnawed at me, but exhaustion soon took its toll. As I lay back on the bed, I could feel the weight of the unknown pressing down on me.

I drifted back into unconsciousness, hoping that when I woke, the pieces of this strange and unsettling puzzle would begin to fit together.

* * *

I tightened my coat around me, trying to ward off the bitingly cold wind as I hurried through the dimly lit streets. Each step seemed to amplify the weight of disappointment that clung to me. The icy air mirrored the emptiness inside me, a sharp contrast to the warmth and excitement I had hoped for my twenty-fifth birthday. Instead, the day had unfolded as a series of letdowns, leaving me feeling lost and alone.

Finally, I reached the dingy bar with its flickering neon sign that boasted Drinks and Snacks, but the lights behind the worn-out *S* had long given up. I pushed through the creaking doors, seeking solace within.

Conversations buzzed around me, filling the air with a low hum as I settled onto a worn stool at the bar. I caught the bartender's attention and let out a weary sigh.

"It's my birthday today. I'm twenty-five," I whispered to him.

He offered me a small, understanding smile. "An auspicious year," he replied gently, his voice laced with kindness. It was the first genuine smile I had encountered all day.

"Let me get you an appropriate drink, on the house," he said, a gesture of compassion threatening to let my dam of tears loose.

As I waited, the memories of my breakup with Tanner flooded my mind. We had dated for two years, and I thought we'd have a future together. But apparently, we "didn't want the same things out of life"—his words, not mine. When I turned eighteen and got a scholarship to college, I thought that by twenty-five, I would have settled down to a good job and a decent life. But here I was, jobless and alone.

Lost in my thoughts, I barely noticed the passage of time as I drowned my sorrows, one drink after another. The bitterness of the alcohol provided a temporary escape from reality, numbing the ache within me. The bar seemed to empty around me, leaving only a handful of people, including the bartender, tidying up for the night.

I glanced at the clock on the far wall—midnight, time to head home.

Gathering my strength, I downed the remnants of my drink and prepared to face the frigid night outside.

As I neared the door, it swung open, a gust of icy wind filling the room. My gaze shifted toward the entrance. A male figure stood on the other side. He turned, scanning the room as if looking for someone, until his eyes met mine.

Time stood still. Dark hair framed a strong jawline, and his eyes, a strange gold that couldn't be natural, held me enraptured. His tall stature cast a shadow that seemed to stretch across the room.

Instinctively, I stepped aside to allow him into the bar.

"He's trouble. Stay away from this one," I murmured.

A slow smile pulled at his lips like he could hear my words. Without warning, he reached out and grabbed me.

"You're coming with me, Starlight," he murmured, his voice laced with irresistible allure. The words reverberated through the air, enveloping me. I opened my mouth to protest, but before a single word could escape, I felt my consciousness slipping as I descended into darkness. Strangely, I felt at peace for the first time today.

* * *

"Wake up."

The command sliced through the remnants of my dream, leaving only fleeting fragments that slipped through my grasp. I blinked my eyes open, trying to shake off the fog of sleep, but my mind remained an enigma, withholding the key to my past.

The voice was different—not the calm tone of my kidnapper. This new voice felt sharp, urgent, and authoritative. Old.

"We have a lot to do."

The words hung in the air, and I realized that my present uncertainty was only matched by the ominous uncertainty of my future.

I blinked, trying to make sense of my surroundings. I was in a dimly lit room, unfamiliar and cold. My heart raced, but I forced myself to stay calm, not wanting to show fear or weakness to whomever this person was.

His eyes. They were the first thing I noticed. They were a dull gray, but they seemed to shift on their own every few seconds, catching the shadows eerily. And they were pinned on me.

Apart from a harsh scar running across his left cheek, there were no other lines on his face, but he was old. Something about his stance and his presence, menacing yet regal, indicated that he was much older than his physique implied.

"Who are you?" I managed to ask, my voice quivering slightly despite my efforts.

"Call me Malachi. All will be revealed in good time," he replied cryptically. "But for now, there are matters we must attend to."

I tried to sit up, but my body felt weak, like I had been through some ordeal. Flashes of my abduction crossed my mind, but I couldn't piece together the details.

"Where am I?" I asked, my voice steadier this time.

"That is not important right now," Malachi said dismissively. "What matters is what comes next."

CHAPTER 2

VENDRICK

I stood at the edge of the Twisted Forest, a malevolence pulsing within its darkness. The creeping decay had transformed this once lush, vibrant woodland into a nightmarish realm.

As the winter solstice approached, the darkness in the realm intensified, and the Twisted Ones grew bolder. The newly formed monsters would venture to the edge of the forest, grabbing anyone who dared come within their reach, any villager—male, female, or youngling—who wandered too far searching for food or firewood. The boundaries of creeping decay expanded slowly, devouring small villages over the course of a decade. However, those in power largely ignored their relentless spread, especially my fellow high and mighty royals, who considered themselves untouchable.

The creatures that emerged from the forest were once Shadowkin-like us. Neither royal nor commoner had been exempted from the corruption that had twisted Shadowkin into monstrous abominations three hundred years ago, except a select few who had remained immune to the threat. There were several opinions on why they were untouchable: some said those connected to the shadows could escape corruption, while others said it was sheer luck or random selection. But no one truly knew why or how.

My heart ached with sorrow and anger as I faced these twisted beings. They had been sentient once, and I loathed the need to destroy them now. Yet I understood the necessity of curbing their threat to civilization; I had witnessed the horrors of the Twisted Forest. Alone most days, I ventured into the dark heart of the woodland, holding back the shadows and fighting to protect the realm from the encroaching malevolence.

As I confronted the first creature to burst out of the forest, I felt the strange bond we shared. The Twisted Ones were drawn to my shadow form, seeking me out as if to embrace me. The creature's limbs contorted at unnatural angles, and its eyes emitted a sinister glow. The stench of decay filled the air, and the ground beneath me was scattered with the remains of its most recent unfortunate victim.

With a deep breath, I summoned my flames. My shadows would only attract more of these creatures, so I relied on the embers to shield me. My eyes blazed with an otherworldly light, my mind focused, and my veins surged with raw power.

A guttural growl escaped its mouth as the twisted creature lunged at me, its claws poised to tear me apart. Swiftly, I dodged the attack, evading the razor-sharp claws that aimed to rend me limb from limb. I thrust my arm forward, aiming for the creature's heart. Brilliant blue flames surged, seeking to destroy it, but the Twisted One swerved with unnatural grace, dodging my attack.

Never faltering, I conjured a fireball, hurling it toward the creature in an attempt to disorient it. It seemed to work for a moment as the Twisted One stared transfixed.

Seizing the opportunity, I moved swiftly, drawing out my throwing stars, infusing them with heat, and launching them at the creature in one smooth motion. Two of them hit home, digging into the surface above the monster's heart. Grunting, it struggled to pull out the stars and tossed them aside before my next attack.

Our battle erupted into a frenzied dance of shadows, fire, and violence. My mind was razor-sharp, anticipating the creature's moves and precisely countering. This was not a newly created Twisted One; he moved with fluid grace. This one was very old, so why was it out on the forest's edge?

Without hesitation, the creature lunged at me with renewed ferocity, catching me off guard. Its claws tore into my side, and I grunted in pain. Blood oozed from the wound, staining my clothes a deep crimson. I pulled out Skjor, my emerald sword, thrusting it at the creature's heart, the blade cutting through the tough skin like water, and the creature let out a final, agonized wail before disintegrating into nothingness.

Exhausted, I sank to my knees, my breath heavy and labored. I could feel the darkness within me receding, leaving me drained and vulnerable. The fight was not over, but the people of the nearby village would be a little safer for a few days.

I had pleaded at length with my father to give me a small army to push back the monsters, but he disregarded the suffering of the common people. Instead, he levied more and more taxes on them for the solstice celebrations.

The royals were safe, which seemed to be all that mattered to the King. It was time to try a different approach.

"There have been two heralded as the Chosen Ones, Uncle. Neither did anything but further separate the Light Court from ours."

I couldn't shake off the feeling of foreboding that settled in my chest. I knew all too well the consequences of involving myself in my uncle's schemes. Malachi always had an ulterior motive and manipulated everyone; if he said one thing, it was wise to assume there were two hidden layers.

Malachi rested a benevolent hand on my shoulder, a sinister smile playing at the corner of his lips. "This one is different. And you need not worry. Your duty ends after you bring her to me."

Not many could walk between the veils that shielded the humans from Shadowkin, and even fewer possessed the ability to take other people with them. I knew that this was the reason why my uncle sought my help. This so-called "Chosen One" was in the human world, and Malachi needed my unique powers to bridge the gap between realms.

I scoffed internally, remembering the failed attempts of the previous Chosen Ones. They had been nothing but pawns in my uncle's grand designs, and I doubted this one would be any different.

As much as I wanted to break free from this arrangement, I couldn't ignore my uncle's looming threat. Malachi schemed to take over the kingdom, gathering an army of discontented royals and commoners whose numbers grew by the day. My father, King Aldric, remained blind to this threat, too consumed by his own obsessions and oblivious to the fate of the entire Shadow Realm.

Someone had to keep an eye on Malachi.

I had seen how my uncle treated the commoners in his army, still harshly but not as cruelly as my father would. It was a twisted form of manipulation that made the commoners believe they had a chance at a better life under Malachi's rule. They were only a means to an end, a fact the commoners didn't seem to understand.

As I stood there, my mind weighed down by these conflicting thoughts, Malachi's voice brought me back to the present. "Bring her to me, Vendrick. She holds the key to our future, and once she's in our grasp, the Shadow Realm will be ours for the taking."

I nodded, my jaw set with determination. I would do what he asked of me this time.

* * *

The veil between realms shimmered and wavered as I stepped through, the familiar sensation of crossing between the Shadow Realm and the human world sending a shiver down my spine. I emerged into a dimly lit street, the cold, damp air immediately enveloping me. The sounds of the bustling city were muted here, replaced by a sense of eerie stillness.

I had arrived at my destination—the human world, a place I seldom visited. My eyes scanned my surroundings, searching for any sign of the one I had been sent to find.

Then, amidst the shadows and dim light, I saw her. She was a few paces away, hastily moving in my direction as she closed her coat against the cold. Even from a distance, there was something about her that captured my attention, an aura that seemed to radiate from her.

Avaline.

I had heard the name before, whispered in hushed tones by my uncle, spoken with reverence and hope. She was the Chosen One, destined to bridge the gap between the Light and Dark Courts, bringing about a new era for our kind.

I observed her intently as she moved, her gaze seeming to flicker in my direction, as if she could tell I was there.

Shadowkin, she was one of us. But why was she here, in the human world?

Her hair, long and dark, cascaded down her back like a waterfall of shadows. Those emerald green eyes caught my attention first, but they seemed dull, like the life had been sucked out of her.

Then, unexpectedly, she turned away, continuing her path without sparing me a second glance. It was as if I was nothing more than a passing shadow in her world, a mere spectator in her life.

Curiosity held me in the shadows as she entered a vile-smelling house that claimed to have snacks and drinks. My concern grew as she kept drinking for hours. I felt an inexplicable desire to walk in there and pull her out, save her from whatever troubled her soul. How could she poison herself so?

As the night deepened, I knew I had to return in time for the final solstice celebrations at the palace; otherwise, my father would question my absence.

I approached the door just as she stood up, turning toward me. Her eyes lit up as they met mine, as though she recognized me. The emerald in her gaze blazed fiercely.

Feeling an unusual pull, I stepped closer to her, captivated by those mesmerizing emerald eyes. It was as if an invisible thread connected us, drawing me in like a moth to a flame.

"He's trouble. Stay away from this one," she muttered under her breath as she stumbled toward me, pulling a small smile out of me.

She was wrong. I was the one that needed to stay away.

CHAPTER 3

AVA

The courtyard was the most beautiful thing I had ever seen. The sky was streaked with hues of blues and purples, and the air felt cleaner than I had ever breathed in my life. The flowers were strange, vibrantly colored, and almost alive. I stepped forward, my head thrown back to admire the breathtaking scenery.

"What time is it?" I asked absentmindedly.

"Ah, about seven bells," Malachi replied.

Seven bells? Who talked like that? It was seven a.m., yet the sun wasn't up. That wasn't how things worked back home. Regardless of the time of year, the sun was always up by seven. What was this place?

I turned around, taking in all I could see, like I'd been starved of beauty all my life. Who knows? Maybe I was.

When I woke up that morning, I found myself in an enormous room adorned in black and gray, a beige dress draped over a sofa at the far end. The dress was my perfect size. Malachi granted me only a brief moment to freshen up, and he stood guard outside my door throughout the time. I knew that none of this was normal, but I felt an unusual urge to ignore the strangeness of it all.

My memories began to trickle in: from the epic disaster that had been my birthday yesterday to my kidnapping, I remembered it all, but none of it felt consequential. I was serene, at peace. Other bits and pieces of my life had been flowing in since I woke up. I was an orphan and had spent most of my life in four different foster homes, but none of it felt very relevant now.

"It's the winter solstice," the man said, interpreting my silence for confusion. "It occurs differently around here, longer, more intense." His voice sounded closer than it was a second ago.

I started. When had he gotten so close?

I turned around sharply. He was standing right behind me, close enough that I could reach out and touch him. He was tall, and I hadn't noticed before, but the other handsome stranger had also been extremely tall. All my life, I'd been taller than most of the men around me, but these two both towered over me. His skin seemed to glow from within, and his long hair was pulled back in a severe bun, exposing long, pointed ears.

"Why am I here?" I asked tentatively. He looked up, a brief flicker of irritation passing over his face, but it passed away easily.

He seemed like a nice person and patient too, but everything in me cautioned me to keep my guard up around him. I was here without my permission, after all, and he seemed to be at the helm of it all. Secondly, all my senses seemed to be in overdrive here. And from this... being, because he very obviously wasn't human, I could detect an undertone of decay. It was very faint, but it was there.

"What do you know about your parents?"

The question stalled me. I had been an orphan for as long as I could remember. Everyone knew that. I had grown up moving from one foster home to the other; it wasn't special anymore. I wasn't the only orphan. But something about how he asked the question made it seem slightly different, like I was about to gain new information about myself.

"I knew your father," Malachi continued, not waiting for my response. "He served in the Dark Court, that is, until he ran away."

Before I could say anything more or ask any of the questions that flooded my mind, he reached out and grabbed my hand, palm up.

I looked down at my hand. I was glowing. I looked around and noticed that even though my vision had always been perfect, everything was sharper now. I could see a strange, colorful bird perched on a tree about a mile away and hear it chirp, too. The same upgrade had happened to my other senses.

I couldn't understand why I was so relaxed, not at all perturbed, even though I'd been kidnapped. It felt like I was in the right place, at least for now. I'd never felt this way all my life; nowhere had felt like home, ever. This wasn't home; I knew that instinctively, but it was the closest I'd come to home my whole life.

Before I could pull my hand back, I felt a vibration start within my veins and spread throughout my hand as if something was being pulled to the surface.

A ball of light floated over my hand. I jerked, trying to pull my hand back, but Malachi would not let go. The light ball was small and flickered away when I finally looked up. Many bizarre things were happening today, and I had no explanation for any of them.

"You are special. More than you know," Malachi said, his voice filled with intensity. "You have a lot to learn, but you have a great destiny, and I will show it to you."

Malachi spent the morning telling me all about the Shadow Realm, the Shadowkin within it, and how I possessed mystic powers. It was all very dizzying, like being plopped right into a fairytale.

We immediately jumped into exercises to help me connect with my "spark of life," whatever that meant. I tried all day, never achieving more than a flimsy speckle of light, no bigger than a firefly. When it finally happened without Malachi touching me, I was overjoyed, but he was not impressed.

"Again!" he bellowed, and I returned to my breathing exercises, trying to connect with my inner strength.

The sun had finally risen but remained at treetop level, moving sluggishly in the sky like a weary traveler, casting long shadows across the land. The winter solstice usually brought a sense of solemnity, as if the world itself paused to reflect on the passing of time, as Malachi had explained. But my concern was that the sun provided very little warmth, and the air held a biting chill.

Just when Malachi decided he couldn't get any more out of me that day, *he* appeared.

One moment he wasn't there, and the next he materialized, the shadows from the nearby tree peeling away from him as though reluctant to let him go. Anger welled in me, shaking me out of the strange calm I had been experiencing since I woke up. Everything seemed crystal clear to me now. He was the enemy, the reason for all of this. He had kidnapped me. Sure, maybe I wasn't having the best life, but nothing gave him the right to uproot me from everything I was familiar with. My life was not his to play with.

The tightly wound ball of essence within me was right there, the one Malachi had been trying to make me envision all day. Except it was not a ball. It was a well and so easy to reach out to it. My essence obeyed my call, streaming through me as easily as the blood in my veins. A ball of light, brighter than I'd conjured with Malachi's help, formed in my palm.

I could see nothing but *him* now. My captor. I wanted to destroy him. I poured my anger—it never seemed to end—into the ball, and it became more solid. Thoughts about how badly I wanted him to hurt, to feel a fraction of the pain I now feel, overwhelmed my mind. The ball of light burst into flames, and I flung it at him with all my might.

He sidestepped easily, moving out of the fireball's trajectory.

The ball landed harmlessly on a grassy hill a few feet behind him, and turning, he doused it with water that he effortlessly conjured using his magic. That angered me even more. But as I tried to conjure another fireball, I discovered that I had lost hold of the stream. It seemed like all my strength and all my fight died instantly, and I collapsed. Before I could reach the ground, my kidnapper was there, holding me.

Looking up at Malachi, accusation and anger marring his beautiful features, he said, "What did you do to her?"

"Emotions, of course," Malachi retorted. "How human. Vendrick Frost, meet Avaline Summers," he went on, gesturing lazily between the both of us. "Although, I suppose you two have already met."

Vendrick, the name suited him perfectly—the prick. Of course, *Vendrick* knew my name; he kidnapped me in the first place! So why did I feel the urge to say his name?

"Vendrick," I blurted out involuntarily, and as he glanced down at me, a teasing grin tugged at his lips, making me instantly regret the slip. However, unconsciousness was rapidly pulling me into its depths, leaving me with no control over the situation.

"At your service, Starlight," he replied.

With that, he lifted me up, carrying me back toward the castle that was now my prison.

CHAPTER 4

VENDRICK

"Why?" I asked, softly closing the door to avoid disturbing Ava, who had fallen asleep in my arms before we entered her room.

Malachi's use of forbidden magic to dampen Ava's emotions troubled me deeply. As much as I tried to understand my uncle's motives, I couldn't fathom why he would resort to such manipulative tactics. We had already kidnapped her, and she had no means of returning to the human world on her own. There seemed to be no need for further manipulation.

Casually flicking his hand in my direction, Malachi seemed dismissive of my objections. "I saw fit," he replied, seemingly unconcerned by the consequences of his actions.

"But it is forbidden," I countered, feeling frustrated and helpless.

He then took an unexpected turn, bringing up the Twisted Forest I frequented to protect the small villages from the twisted creatures. It was as if he knew my every move and intention. The notion sent a chill down my spine, reminding me of the constant surveillance I lived under in the Dark Realm.

"I need one of the Twisted Ones, alive but weakened," he stated plainly, and I instinctively pulled my shadows closer around me, uneasy about his request.

"She's very human," I emphasized, my protectiveness of Ava welling up. "You cannot subject her to a Twisted One! She was barely aware of our existence yesterday. Are you trying to destroy her?"

Despite my protest, Malachi seemed unmoved, insisting that she must be ready in time for his mysterious plans. My resolve strengthened; I would not let him harm her.

"You cannot do this," I firmly stated, refusing to comply with his dark intentions. "I will not get you a Twisted One."

"Very well," he replied nonchalantly after a moment's contemplation. "I don't need you for that task. Your duty lies elsewhere. I need you to return to your father with a message from me."

Annoyance and anger swirled inside me. I was not his errand boy, and his demands were testing the limits of my loyalty. I couldn't allow him to cross the line and become even worse than my father, the current ruler. If that happened, I would not hesitate to end his tyranny myself.

"Calm yourself, Vendrick," he patronized, his tone dripping with condescension. "I am not trying to antagonize you. Someone needs to confront your father about taming that forest. If he continues to hide in his castle, the Twisted Ones will overrun him after they're done with the commoners. What then?"

His words gave me pause. He had a point, and though I despised Malachi's authoritative manner, I couldn't ignore the danger posed by the unchecked Twisted Ones. Reluctantly, I nodded, realizing that this task was not solely for Malachi's benefit but for the greater good of the realm.

"I will deliver your message, but that is the extent of my involvement," I asserted firmly.

I hated both of them—my father and Malachi. King Aldric refused to listen to my pleas once he realized that I wanted to talk about the Twisted Forest. Apparently, my news was dampening the winter solstice celebrations.

Malachi was equally despicable.

I stared at the broken body of the monstrous creature lying on the ground in the cellar and then turned to look at Ava, who had folded in on herself and was shivering in the corner.

Anger surged within me as I faced Malachi, pulling us into a curtain of shadows to protect Ava from what was about to happen. Malachi shifted to a more alert stance as he faced me. The tension in the air was palpable as we squared off, ready to confront each other.

"It was necessary!" Malachi insisted. "We've already accomplished more within minutes than in the last four days."

"Look at her! Look at what you're doing to her!"

"Yes, look," Malachi replied calmly. "She did that. Destroyed it within mere moments," he concluded, motioning for me to lower the Shadow curtain.

Reluctantly, I complied and looked at Ava again, noticing something I had missed before. She wasn't shivering in fear as I'd thought before. Instead, she seemed to be glowing with newfound strength, her determination shining through.

"She's stronger than I realized," I muttered, my voice tinged with awe and surprise.

"I told you she's special," Malachi said, a hint of satisfaction in his voice. "And now you see it for yourself. She possesses powers beyond anything we've seen in a long time."

But my wonder quickly turned to concern as I saw a deep, dark cut running across her arm from where the Twisted One had dug its claws into her.

A mixture of emotions churned within me, conflicting loyalties pulling me in different directions. For some reason, I was fiercely protective of Ava. The thought of her in pain caused my chest to constrict. On the other hand, I was fascinated by her strength and potential. The Twisted One had burned from the inside out. There were very few Shadowkin in the realm who could wield such power with so little practice. I still didn't want to believe anything about a Chosen One, but Malachi was right; she was special.

I hurried to her, turning her arm around in my hands. The wounds were already closing on their own, which surprised me: only the Shadowkin of old had that ability. I removed the scarf around my neck, tying it around her injury and using her other hand to apply pressure.

"I won't let you use her like a pawn in your games," I declared to my uncle, my voice firm with resolve. "She deserves better than that."

Malachi's expression turned cold and calculating. "She is the Chosen One, Vendrick," he said. "Destiny has brought her here for a reason. We cannot ignore it."

"Destiny did nothing. You both did. You uprooted me from my life and brought me here." The strength in Ava's voice as she spoke drew my attention.

"She's right," I concurred softly as our eyes met. "The least we can do is be responsible for her."

However, I knew Malachi was right. She was supposed to be here.

Before I could ponder further, a loud crash echoed through the cellar as another Twisted One burst through the doors, drawn by the commotion. This time, there was no time to hesitate. I had to protect Ava.

"How many did you get?" I growled at Malachi, reaching for Skjor.

"Enough," he replied simply before pinning the Twisted One to the wall with wind and beheading it with a dagger in one fluid motion. "If you can do a better job, then take over her training."

I hesitated for a moment, torn between my resolve not to get too involved in Malachi's scheming and my growing desire and fascination with Ava. But I couldn't let my emotions cloud my judgment. She needed guidance and protection, and I was determined to be the one to provide it.

"You will train me, Vendrick," Ava interrupted, "You owe me that much."

"I will," I replied, her amazing resilience strengthening my resolve.

"I won't be a pawn," she announced to Malachi as she stood up and straightened her clothes. "I have a lot to learn, but I make my own choices."

Malachi's eyes narrowed, but he seemed to accept her decision. "Very well, then," he said, a hint of something unreadable in his gaze. "I'll leave you both to it."

CHAPTER 5

AVA

Vendrick and I stood quietly in the castle courtyard, watching Malachi leave, when suddenly, my memories returned in a rush, overwhelming me with all the emotions I had been shielded from for days. The anger, frustration, and pain hit me like a tidal wave triggered by the spell that had dampened my emotions. Vendrick had warned me this would happen, but experiencing it firsthand was still shocking.

As the overwhelming emotions threatened to consume me, I felt a desperate need for release. I couldn't contain them anymore; they were like a turbulent storm raging within, ready to tear me apart. I conjured the hottest fireball I had ever created. It was small but intense, fueled by the turmoil inside me. I flung it at Vendrick, filled with rage and hatred for everything he had taken from me. To my surprise, he didn't dodge the attack; he let it strike him in the chest. The fire consumed his clothes and singed his skin, but he remained standing, sweat forming on his brow.

I hated him and blamed him for my pain.

Kill him, a voice whispered inside me. *It will all go away when he dies.*

The idea was horrifying, but in that moment of desperation, it seemed like the only solution. I had to kill him; the voice was right.

Channeling all my emotions, I intensified the fireball, drilling it deeper into Vendrick's chest. An evil smile cut across my face. He would pay!

He cried out in pain, dropping to the floor, trying to extinguish the flames. I had never seen him so vulnerable, which made me question my actions.

Why wasn't he fighting back?

As suddenly as it came, the haze of anger lifted inside me, and panic and remorse flooded in. I rushed to his side, pressing my hands over the mangled hole in his chest, horrified by the damage I'd caused. What had come over me? Why would I do that?

After college, I spent 6 months as an EMT before I decided that I didn't want to have that many lives depending on me when I barely knew how to take care of myself. I tried to remember my training as an EMT so that I could help him, but I didn't know if it would work. His body differed from a human's, but I hoped it wouldn't matter. I started CPR anyway.

"Don't die. I'm sorry, I didn't mean it. Please, wake up," I pleaded, tears streaming down my face. I kept performing chest compressions, desperate to save him. But as time passed, I felt a sense of helplessness creeping in.

Vendrick. He was the one who had saved me from Malachi's monsters, the only one who had shown me care and kindness in this strange world. I couldn't let him die.

Without him, I was alone.

"Please!" I cried out, refusing to give up. "Come back!"

And then, a croaking voice emerged from under my hands. "Chosen One." Relief washed over me as Vendrick spoke. He sat up, robbing at the burned spot, which was disappearing.

He was alive. I collapsed in his arms, relieved and overwhelmed with emotion.

"Starlight, I'm here," he murmured, his arms holding me tightly. He rubbed small circles on my back, comforting me. "I'm here, and I'm not going anywhere."

I clung to him, feeling a deep connection despite everything that had happened between us. He was the only one who seemed to be on my side, the only one who cared for me in this unfamiliar realm.

"I didn't mean to hurt you," I whispered, my voice shaking with remorse.

Vendrick lifted my chin, making me meet his gaze. "I know," he said softly. "It's not your fault. Malachi used his powers to stifle your emotions. Not many can do that."

Cold shivers ran up my spine as I realized the reach of Malachi's powers. I didn't know how, but I had to make sure Malachi could never do that to me again — make me hurt people around me. I could start by learning to control my powers.

"You are strong, Ava, but you cannot kill me yet," Vendrick quipped as he watched me.

His calmness about this frustrated me, and I lashed out at him. I couldn't understand why he hadn't defended himself. He calmly caught my fists, effortlessly stopping my assault. His snarky smile only fueled my irritation further.

"Why didn't you fight back?" I yelled, my voice trembling with emotion.

He regarded me with a cool expression, seemingly unaffected by my outburst. "You're glowing," he stated matter-of-factly, as if it were an everyday observation.

I glanced down at my hands, and sure enough, a soft, ethereal glow emanated from my skin.

"Good. Now, let's get to work, Chosen One," he continued, his tone dripping with sarcasm.

"Again," Vendrick called from the top of the overturned crate he had converted into a platform.

I sighed and moved into the stance he'd shown me earlier – to improve my balance, he'd said, and I prepared to summon my light.

Vendrick was annoyed with me. He had to be, even though he was never rough, and he didn't snap at me like his uncle did. Over the past week, my progress had been frustratingly slow, and I knew it disappointed him. Today was no different, and I felt the weight of my inability to control the globe of light without adding any heat to it. I managed to do it briefly, but my control faltered almost immediately.

"Try harder. Concentrate." His words echoed in my mind like a constant reminder of my shortcomings.

And then there were those vague statements that were supposed to be encouraging but fell flat.

"You lack faith in your abilities." He said in a matter-of-fact tone.

I winced inwardly every time he said that. Not because he was wrong but because he had unknowingly touched on a more profound insecurity. I remembered the darkness lurking within me; I had almost killed him. Maybe my powers were evil and destructive and should be left dormant.

"I can't," I muttered, my spirits sinking as I plopped down on the grass. "I'm done for today. I'll go and clean up for dinner."

Vendrick jumped down from the makeshift platform and walked over to where I sat. "Yes, you can. But meanwhile, I'll believe on your behalf." And with that, he tapped my ankles gently before straightening again.

"Don't be late for dinner," he threw over his shoulder as he walked away.

Every evening, we would share dinner, one of my favorite times of the day in this strange castle. Breakfast was always waiting for me in the outer chamber of my room when I woke up. It consisted of dishes I had loved growing up, though I had no idea where they came from. Yet, it was always delicious, and I woke up starving, eager to devour the meal. Lunch usually consisted of packed leftovers from breakfast and some fruit. But dinner was different, a grand affair.

We dined in the gigantic dining room downstairs, which could easily seat twenty people. However, we always chose to sit next to each other, right in the middle of the table. It was during these dinners that Vendrick would open up and truly talk to me.

At first, I bombarded him with questions, desperate to understand why he called me the Chosen One, why I was here, and if he was a faery. I wanted to know if time passed differently here. He told me about the prophecy of the Chosen One, who was destined to restore balance to the realm. He also said that Malachi seemed convinced that I was the Chosen One. Yet, he emphasized that he didn't believe any of it. As for why I was here, he didn't know, but he seemed glad that I was.

They were Shadowkin, and they belonged to two Courts – the Light and Dark Courts. We were in the Dark Court, and Vendrick was Dark Shadowkin. He was convinced I was Light Shadowkin because of my light magic, but he wasn't sure there wasn't more.

The two kingdoms were separated by the Forbidden Forest, which was filled with Twisted Ones — former Shadowkin twisted by a magic curse — the ones Malachi had attacked me with. He was still angry about that. He didn't say so, but his voice hardened as he spoke.

The word "home" felt foreign to me. I had never had a home, but this empty, dreary castle with him in it was becoming the closest thing to it. And I couldn't deny that he was the reason for it. He hadn't known what a faery was, which I found amusing.

The food was always waiting on the table when I came down after refreshing from our daily training. When I asked him where the food came from, he growled, "Eat." I had a habit of making him taste the food before I ate any of it, which amused him every time. According to him, poison was considered a female's weapon in the Dark Realm.

As the days passed, he began to offer information unprompted. He told me about the Dark Court and last night, he told me about himself—how he was the second son of the King of the Dark Realm, and that Malachi was his uncle.

A prince. Now that was fitting, and his grumpy, high and mighty behavior finally made sense. I couldn't help but roll my eyes at this revelation.

With an intense stare that made me blush, he said, "Do that again, and I will not be responsible for my actions."

He issued a threat, but the heat that surged through my body surprised me. I bit my lip, leaning into him. There was something between us. I could see the heat in his golden eyes and the flecks of brown I hadn't noticed before. I reached out my hand to touch his silken hair. He was so close, and it was as if I couldn't control my own actions. My lips met his in a soft, trance-like kiss.

"Ava," my name, soft as a prayer, fell from his lips as he deepened the kiss. He lifted me from my chair onto his lap, his hands exploring my hair, and my neck, drifting down to my shoulders, his lips trailing kisses across my cheeks and down my neck, drawing a soft sigh from my throat.

The sound seemed to snap him out of the trance, and he returned me to my chair with an apology. Then he got up swiftly and left the room without another word.

The shock of his exit kept me glued to my chair long after he left. The details of everything that happened replayed in my mind as I tried to think through everything that just happened. And what I could have done differently.

My fingers flew to my lips the next morning as I bolted out of bed. The memory of the kiss still brought heat to my face as I distractedly stepped outside my room.

"Oof."

I ran into Vendrick's substantial, warm chest. He was right outside my door. *What was he doing here?* I tried to pull away, unsure about where things were with us, considering the rapid end of our meeting yesterday. But he held me in place, prolonging the hug for just a little longer before pulling away.

"Come with me. I want to show you something," Vendrick whispered softly, still holding onto my hand.

CHAPTER 6

VENDRICK

I *never wanted to let her go.*

The thought settled in my mind as I walked to Ava's room.

Every day since that night in the human realm, I was drawn to Ava. The harder I tried, the harder it became. I was unable to resist her magnetic presence. The way her eyes sparkled when she learned something new and the warmth of her smile—they all captivated me.

The kiss we had shared yesterday, however, was different. It had stirred something deeper within me, something stronger, darker—I wanted her to be mine.

Long before last night, I had decided that it would be enough if I remained by her side, protecting and guiding her in her training. But now, all of that was about to change.

Her progress with her powers was remarkable, and I admired her determination to master them. However, she still struggled with controlling the intensity and duration of her light manipulations. But she needed an extra push. I knew that showing her the Dark Realm's dire state and the people depending on her would motivate her to strengthen her powers.

I reached for the door handle when it opened, and she barreled into me. She was in my arms once more, and for a moment, I felt whole. I longed to wrap my arms around her and keep her there forever.

"Come with me," I said, taking her hand gently in mine. "I have something to show you."

As we walked through the castle grounds, I lifted the wards to allow her to pass through easily. Her shoulders hunched involuntarily as she stepped out, and I put a hand on the small of her back to remind her that she was not alone. I was here. I would not leave her. With a deep breath, she stepped forward.

As we headed toward the village near the Twisted Forest, we heard a faint whimpering noise in the bushes. Ava perked up, her instincts guiding her toward the sound. We found an injured shadow wolf bleeding from a deep claw wound on its side.

Without hesitation, Ava knelt and cradled the pup in her arms, her voice soothing and gentle as she murmured to it. The pup seemed to respond to her, quieting down as she reassured it. I watched in awe as she glowed, and the wound on the pup's side vanished, the bleeding stopping.

"You saved him, Starlight," I said, lifting her face to mine. Her face was now tear-stained.

She looked at me with shining eyes, holding the pup close to her. "He needed help, and I couldn't just leave him there."

My heart swelled with affection for her, and I couldn't help but hug her tightly, planting a soft kiss on her forehead. "I know. Do you want to head back home?" I asked gently, concern evident in my voice.

"No, the monster that did this is still on the loose," she replied, her determination returning. "The villagers are nearby, aren't they?"

I nodded, impressed by her bravery and sense of responsibility. "Yes. Let's go help them."

The village was in flames.

Terrified villagers were fleeing in every direction. Twisted Ones roamed the streets, causing chaos and destruction. This was not supposed to be possible; they couldn't, shouldn't be able to come out of the Twisted Forest, and definitely not during the daylight. Or in this number. They weren't sentient or organized enough for that.

Ava could not be here. I tried to persuade Ava to leave the village, but she was determined to ensure every monster was destroyed.

Without further hesitation, Ava sprang into action, using her newfound powers to protect the villagers. She summoned her light weapons and shields, driving back the Twisted Ones and providing a safe passage for the villagers to escape. She blazed with ethereal light as she tossed fireball after fireball at the monsters who approached her. Drawing Skjor, and with my back to hers, I plunged into the fight, slashing at every one of the monsters that dared to come close to her.

For hours, we fought tirelessly, driving the creatures back into the forest.

I lunged, stabbing a creature that reached for her. My blade found its heart and turned it to dust just as Ava's eyes widened at something behind me. Motioning for me to duck, she sent one of her fireballs into a Twisted One that had come too close to me.

As soon as the fight was over, there was an earsplitting scream from one of the women villagers.

"My son! No, help him, please!"

Ava had begun to stagger after using so much power, but the woman's desperate cries for help drew her attention. She ran toward the source of the distress. The boy was going through violent shudders, foaming at the mouth already. The mother struggled to keep him still, but she wouldn't succeed much longer.

I hurried to help contain the boy and find the bite. Once bitten by a Twisted One, the only way to save the person was to treat it like a snake bite. The site had to be isolated immediately. The poison from the monster's venom colonized the cells in the area within minutes. Once the area turned blue, the person could no longer be saved.

The bite was already a deep blue hue. We were too late. I moved back and reached for Ava to pull her away.

I tried to explain that there was nothing we could do once the change to a Twisted One began, but Ava seemed transfixed, her glowing hand extended toward the boy.

"It won't do any good," I said softly, trying to convince her to step back. "Healers have tried everything before, but he is beyond saving. The kindest thing we can do now is end his suffering."

The mother moaned painfully at my words, but Ava was oblivious. Her eyes had glazed over, her glowing hands still over the boy. Suddenly, he stopped moving, and I feared the worst. But then, to our astonishment, he coughed, and dark tendrils poured from his mouth.

He opened his eyes, calling out to his mother. "Mama?"

The woman sobbed with relief. "Chosen One, thank you."

She attempted to kneel before Ava, still cradling her son, but Ava reached out, stopping her.

"I'm glad your son is alright," Ava whispered.

The exertion had taken its toll on Ava, and she collapsed in exhaustion. I caught her before she hit the ground. I was not taking her back to the castle; there was no doubt in my mind now that she was the Chosen One, and I needed to keep her away from Malachi and his schemes. Gently cradling her in my arms, I assured the grateful mother that Ava would be all right.

"I was right this time," a familiar voice said calmly.

I looked up from Ava's comatose body.

"Your part is done, Vendrick. You have trained her beautifully. I'll take over from here."

Malachi stood at the road leading out of the village, his soldiers blocking every exit point. I tensed, calculating my next move. There were at least forty soldiers. I couldn't fight them all, but I had to try. I couldn't just hand her over to Malachi.

"I've told you, Malachi, I won't let her be a pawn in your games."

Malachi's laughter tore at me as I set Ava down as gently as possible and prepared to fight for us both.

CHAPTER 7

Ava

I groaned and slowly opened my eyes, blinking away the blurriness. Malachi's smirking face came into focus, and I immediately felt a surge of anger and fear. I was in my room again, in my bed, but this time, my hands were tied on either side of the bedpost. I tried to sit up, but my head throbbed with pain, and I winced.

"Don't move too quickly, Chosen One," Malachi said, his voice dripping with false concern. "You've exerted quite a bit of power."

I glared at him; my hands clenched into fists. "What do you want?"

Malachi chuckled, his eyes gleaming with malice. "Oh, so many things, my dear," he replied. "But first, I propose a deal."

"I will never work with you!" I spat.

"There is darkness within you, little one. It calls to you," Malachi replied, ignoring my outburst. I swallowed hard, trying to ignore the rising panic within me. I knew he was right. There was so much I didn't understand about my powers, and I was still struggling to control them.

"But fear not," Malachi continued, his tone sinister. "I am here to guide you. Embrace the darkness within you, and together, we will unlock your true potential."

I shook my head, rejecting his offer. "I will never work with you," I asserted firmly.

Malachi's smile faded, and his expression turned cold. "You're a fool," he spat. "You have no idea what you're rejecting. I'm taking over the Dark Court. Vendrick has nothing to offer you!"

Vendrick. He had been with me at the village. He wouldn't have abandoned me.

"Where is Vendrick?" I asked, trying to keep my voice composed.

A menacing smile crept across Malachi's face.

"Do what I ask, and you will see him again," Malachi said, a sinister gleam in his eyes.

I hesitated, torn between my fear for Vendrick's safety and my determination not to succumb to Malachi's will. But I couldn't let anything happen to Vendrick; I had to protect him, even if it meant making a deal with the devil himself.

"What do you want?" I asked, my voice steady.

CHAPTER 8

VENDRICK

T he castle was crawling with Malachi's soldiers.

I slipped in through the shadows, slashing at one of the soldiers, and blinding the other with more shadow, followed swiftly by my knife. Before they dropped to the ground, I was already moving. Malachi had set his guards all around the castle grounds, but they would not keep me away. I had to get Ava back.

They had overwhelmed me at the village, only keeping me down long enough for Malachi and his goons to leave with Ava. My heart ached every time I thought of her. Malachi would not hurt her. He needed her for his plans.

Suddenly, loud thuds came from the front door. "Open in the name of the King!" The King's Guard was here.

My father never liked to be out of the loop for very long. And I was sure he'd already gotten the information about what had happened back in the village already. So, it was no surprise that the King's Guard was here, but it was fortunate. I could leave Malachi's soldiers to them. I had other business.

CHAPTER 9

AVA

My options were clear: succumb to Malachi's will or lose Vendrick. Weeks ago, I would have walked away from it all without looking back. That was how I had lived my entire life, after all. But in such a short time, this Shadow Realm had become my home. Back in the human realm, I had nothing—no family and very few friends. Nobody probably even noticed I was gone. But here, as the Chosen One, I had value. I had done the impossible by stopping that little boy from transforming into one of those twisted monsters. Here, I had real power.

And then, there was Vendrick. Yes, he had kidnapped me at first, but things had changed since then. I knew now that he regretted it, even though it had felt like the right thing when Malachi had given the command. But he had owned up to his wrongdoing. The best part was the fact that since I got here, he had gone on to do everything in his capacity to make sure I didn't come into further harm.

Now I had begun to see my life here as a gift, a new chance at life. And Vendrick had become my friend, my partner, my unwavering supporter. He never held me back; instead, he believed in me and saw me for who I truly was. He could be grumpy and aloof, but he also stood up to Malachi on my behalf when he could have walked away. He believed in my abilities more than I did, and he made sure I knew it, too, while he drove me hard during our training. Then he'd make me dinner and ensure I never felt alone. We shared a connection on a soul level that I couldn't explain.

When we went to the village, I saw a different side of him—one that cared deeply about the people. They knew him and respected him. It was clear that he had what it took to be a ruler, to lead with both strength and compassion.

And then, there was that kiss...

The memory of that kiss made my heart race and my face flush. It had been innocent and sweet, but it had stirred something inside me, something I hadn't fully understood until now. I think I'm falling in love with him.

There was a magnetic pull between us, a connection that I couldn't ignore. Yet, I was afraid to admit my feelings. What if it was all one-sided? What if he only saw me as the Chosen One and nothing more?

"No," I finally said to Malachi, my voice firm and resolute. "The choice you offer is no choice at all. If I choose your path, I lose Vendrick too."

The more I spoke, the more confident I became. Malachi needed me, and I was sure that if he had Vendrick, he would have brought him here to increase the pressure. Vendrick was safe then. All I needed to do was hold on a little longer as I figured out how to escape.

Malachi's eyes darkened, and he took a step closer, his face inches from mine. "You leave me no choice then."

He drew back, and I closed my eyes, bracing, ready for whatever was coming next. But it never came.

CHAPTER 10

VENDRICK

M alachi knew I was coming. There was no other explanation for this. All the rooms in the castle were spelled to look the same, a calculated effort to disorient and confuse me. As I shadow-shifted through each room, frustration and desperation gripped my heart. Where was she? If he was going to such lengths to mask her from me, something was seriously wrong. Fear gnawed at the edges of my mind; I needed to find her, and fast.

Exhausted, I collapsed against a nearby wall. Confusion, anger, and frustration raged through me like a relentless storm. I ran my hand through my hair, trying to think clearly amidst the chaos inside my mind.

And then I felt it—a thread of connection, so faint yet so unmistakably hers. A thread of pure light, her essence. It had been there all along, waiting for me to grasp it. With newfound determination, I reached into my mind's eye, grabbing onto that thread. As the shadows parted, there she was, tied up in her bed. Anger blazed like wildfire within me, intensified by the realization that she was my mate, my other half, and no one had the right to hurt her.

"If I chose your path, I would lose Vendrick too." Her words echoed in my mind, and strangely, they soothed the rage that threatened to consume me. Her voice grounded me, reminding me of who I was and what we meant to each other. But Malachi's following words sent chills down my spine.

Without hesitation, I sprang into action, covering the distance between me and Malachi in a heartbeat. But he was ready for me. A bolt of darkness, like a poisoned shard, launched at me, catching me in the chest before I could even react. The pain was searing, and the darkness clawed at my very soul, trying to take hold of me.

A feral scream erupted from Ava's lips. A blinding light burst forth from her, engulfing the room in a radiant glow. The power emanating from her pushed back the darkness that sought to engulf us.

Ava's light blazed like a supernova, and then she was free; her bonds turned to ashes. Through my pain, I felt her in my mind. A light strand, blazing bright as she was physically, stretched out in my direction. An answering dark strand started from me towards her.

Mate, I was now positive she was my mate, as her light wrapped around my hanging dark strand. The strands were changing to become one, the light and dark dancing around each other. Light seeped into me through the bond, holding back the flood of darkness threatening to swallow me.

CHAPTER 11

AVA

Vendrick was hurt, and it tore at my heart. Something had happened; we were connected in a way I couldn't explain now. I saw in my mind's eye the bond that started from me and extended to him. It swirled and hummed powerfully within me. The bond settled in me, filling me with strength and determination. I knew I had to protect him, to avenge the one who had dared to harm him.

With little thought, a sword materialized in my hand, its name coming to me effortlessly—Dawnbreaker, as if it had existed for ages, waiting for this very moment.

I turned to face Malachi, his menacing presence still lingering. Without hesitation, I lunged forward, aiming to plunge the sword through his heart. But as it pierced through his chest, he vanished. My fury was unsatisfied, but I knew that I would find him and make him pay for what he'd done.

As I released the sword, it dissipated into the ether, but I felt its power lingering within me and knew I could conjure it again whenever needed.

However, my immediate concern was Vendrick. I rushed to his side, holding his hands tightly, trying to heal his wounds and banish the darkness that had taken hold of him.

"You were magnificent, Starlight," he croaked, but I ignored him, focusing solely on finding and removing the source of his torment.

"Mine! He is mine!" I screamed, frustration and determination fueling my efforts as I snipped away at the tendrils of darkness that had ensnared him. With every strand I severed, his body began to respond, the gaping wound in his chest slowly closing.

"Yours..." he smiled weakly, his voice barely a whisper. "I'm yours."

The confession sent warmth spreading through my heart. I cradled his lying form, and he brought his arms around me, pulling me in a warm embrace.

"My mate, I found you," Vendrick whispered.

Mate, the word resonated and settled in me. He was my mate.

I couldn't tell how long we'd stayed like that when the door suddenly banged open. "The King demands your presence, Chosen One," the captain of the King's Guard announced as he entered the room.

I raised my head. "I will see the King," I replied, "but in my own time."

From now on, my focus was on my happiness. *I* shaped my future and destiny. I would not answer to another manipulative figure like Malachi.

"Leave, Gerald. We will see the King in the morning after we have gathered our strength," Vendrick added when the Guard didn't budge at my words. After hesitating long enough to take one last look at us, the captain – Gerald – turned and left the room.

I turned back to look at Vendrick as I followed the sounds of even strides of the Captain's retreat. He was smiling at me.

"My mate, my perfect, brilliant mate." He pulled me to him, raising his head, his lips meeting mine in a searing kiss. The world around us faded away as our mouths moved in perfect sync. It was a dance of passion and desire, each movement fueled by our intense connection.

My fingers tangled in his dark hair, pulling him closer and deepening the kiss. Vendrick's arms wrapped around my waist, pulling me flush against him. The heat between our bodies was intoxicating as I melted into his embrace.

This was my life now, and I was going to make the most of it.

CHAPTER 12

VENDRICK

For the first time in all my life, I woke up feeling complete.

The sun painted the sky with hues of gold and rose as the morning light filtered through the curtains of the room. I watched Ava stir in her sleep. The events of the previous day were still fresh in my mind. The victory, the intense battle, and the overpowering relief that flooded me when it was finally over. Ava's incredible strength through it all.

I turned my head to watch as she slept peacefully, her features relaxed in slumber. A small smile tugged at my lips, my heart swelling with affection, remembering the night we spent making love.

Mate, she was my mate, and she was incredible.

She fought for me, with me yesterday. *She* protected me. And she accepted me. She was my ally, and our rough beginning was now a thing of the past.

With a gentle sigh, Ava shifted closer, her body instinctively seeking the warmth of mine even in her sleep. I reached out and pulled her flush against me as her eyes fluttered open. The corners of my lips quirked into a sleepy smile as her gaze met mine.

"Good morning," she murmured, her voice husky with sleep.

"Good morning, Starlight."

Ava blinked awake, instantly more attentive. "Why do you call me Starlight, though?"

I chuckled, planting a tender kiss on her forehead. "Starlight is the ultimate light magic— it is the only thing that can create life from nothing. It can also obliterate anything. Only gods can wield it; no Shadowkin can endure its force."

"When we first met, your powers hadn't bloomed, but I sensed that you were about to change me irrevocably" I admitted, a hint of awe in my voice.

She grinned. "I really like that."

There was a raw vulnerability to her as our eyes met, an intimacy that came from facing the shadows together. Ava's breath caught as I stretched, my muscles flexing as I moved her on top of me. A mischievous grin played at my lips as her eyes ran down my bare chest.

Her gaze roamed my chest, and her delicate fingers followed the path her eyes traced. As her touch grazed the scar near my heart, a tangible reminder of Malachi's vicious attack, her fingers hesitated, a shadow crossing over her expression, and her fist clenched in response.

"You saved me," I breathed, my voice a tender murmur as I drew her closer. "That scar is a testament to our beginning, not a reminder of darkness but a symbol of triumph."

The scar that could have been a symbol of my undoing now was a badge of our shared strength, a mark of how love had conquered despair. It was the kind of story that would echo through generations, a narrative of love's unwavering power pulling one back from the brink of destruction.

A surge of emotion filled me as Ava lowered herself, her lips placing soft, tender kisses along the scar's path. Her whispered vow, spoken between each kiss, resonated through me. "Never again," she pledged, her words weaving a cocoon of protection around us both.

Desire, always smoldering between us, ignited into a blazing inferno. With an urgency that matched the fire in our hearts, I pulled her closer until there was no space between us. Our lips met in a fervent, hungry kiss, a meeting of souls as much as a collision of mouths.

Ava's fingers found their way into my tousled hair, her possessive and tender touch as if she sought to anchor herself to me. The world around us faded into insignificance as our bodies pressed against each other, the heat between us driving us to a point of no return.

We struggled to get closer to each other. Her kisses were hungry now. They trailed from my lips to my neck and down my throat, pulling a groan out of me.

This woman would be my undoing. I flipped her over so I could take a good look at her.

Her body flushed with desire as she moved up the bed and crooked her finger, summoning me. I crawled up her, leaving a trail of kisses and little love bites until I'd explored every inch of her perfect form. She was breathless and squirming by the time my lips met her throat.

"Vendrick, please!"

A little gasp left her, and I shivered as I nudged her entrance.

I thrust deep, the sensation already overwhelming because of the link between our minds. I felt everything, the stretch, the burn, her absolute pleasure in addition to my own.

"Oh gods, Ava," I groaned.

I rocked into her, then pulled out to the tip before sinking fully into her once more. Then, hovering over her, I stared hard at the woman I loved, watching her eyes glaze over as need took her closer to climax.

Her thoughts reached me, her voice as clear in my mind as if she'd whispered in my ear.

God, Vendrick, you feel so good.

I roared her name, my hands fisting in her hair and holding her in place as my body shuddered with the intensity of my release.

As I recovered, her voice whispered in my mind once more. *Mine.*

My heart swelled, and I knew nothing would ever be the same now.

Until this moment, I'd lived solely for myself. And now, I existed only for her.

* * *

We had slept again, tangled in each other's arms. As I stirred from slumber, I found her gaze fixed upon me, her eyes already awake and alight with an affectionate intensity.

"Admiring your handiwork?" I quipped playfully.

A soft chuckle escaped her lips before she responded, her tone equally lighthearted. "Indeed, and I must say, I quite like what I see."

Bending closer, I captured her forehead in a tender kiss, a gentle touch that conveyed more than words ever could. In that lingering connection, amidst the quiet moments of the morning, our bond felt deeper and more profound than ever before.

"You were incredible yesterday," I told her, my eyes locked onto hers.

Ava's cheeks warmed at the praise, her gaze never wavering from mine. "So were you," she replied, her voice barely more than a breath.

Suddenly, her posture shifted, and a more serious expression settled on her face. "The Twisted Ones weren't supposed to be capable of what they did at the village yesterday, were they?"

Her words struck a chord deep within me, echoing the concerns that had lingered since our last encounter with Malachi. The Twisted Ones had never exhibited such coordination before.

"Could Malachi have exerted some form of control over them?" Her question hung in the air, laden with implications that sent a chill down my spine.

Malachi was a powerful enough shadow-wielder that he could manipulate the very essence of the Twisted One's darkness residing within them. The audacity of such manipulation had been tested before, though never without dire consequences.

I went on to tell Ava the story of Malroth, the only Shadowkin who'd had done it successfully. He was the most powerful shadow-wielder of his time. He had tried to use the Twisted Ones for his own purposes. He unleashed them on whoever offended him. But the corruption had eaten him from the inside, turning him into a monster worse than the Twisted Ones.

Malroth's tale had become a cautionary whisper passed from mother to child, a narrative woven to dissuade the young from treading the path of wickedness. His name was invoked to remind those who were tempted about what awaited those who ventured too far into the Twisted Forest.

Ava's gaze held a mix of fascination and trepidation as she absorbed the story.

There wasn't much we could do to save Malachi if he had indeed decided to go down that path. We could only prepare ourselves to thwart his plans when he inevitably made his next move.

Amid the heavy atmosphere, Ava's voice rose once more, tinged with panic. "I can't believe I said that to the King's men!" Her words carried a mixture of incredulity and anxiety.

I chuckled softly as I attempted to calm her with soft strokes down her arm.

"He had it coming," I snorted. "If this kingdom wants a Chosen One, they'll have to learn to work with her, not the other way around."

"Thank you for being here for me," Ava whispered, her brilliant eyes reflecting the depth of her emotions.

I smiled. "Always," I said, my voice a promise that resonated deep within us through the bond.

CHAPTER 13

Ava

This was the most beautiful and impossible work of architecture I had ever seen.

I stood in the courtyard, struggling to keep my mouth from falling agape, my brain working overtime to comprehend the sheer grandeur of the palace of the Dark Court. It was a sight that surpassed imagination, and it left me both awed and apprehensive.

The walls of the palace, encircled by a formidable wall, rose like ancient sentinels. Each stone seemed to have been chiseled into shape by the hands of giants, their sheer size and weight a testament to the craftsmanship that had birthed this architectural wonder. The stones were dark as if they absorbed the shadows that danced around the palace. Carvings of intricate patterns adorned the walls, like the markings of an ancient language. There was an eerie beauty to their arrangement, like a forgotten melody in a haunting tune.

In the heart of the courtyard, my gaze swept across an expanse of polished obsidian stone tiles, cool and smooth underfoot. The courtyard itself was meticulously arranged with lush greenery that contrasted sharply with the foreboding stone walls. Flowers with vibrant green vines and purple flowers wound their way amidst the dark stones, adorning the palace with a spark of life and color that was unexpected yet oddly fitting. They seemed to thrive despite the darkness that enveloped the palace. Fountains adorned with onyx sculptures cast a gentle melody as water cascaded and pooled into reflective basins. The air carried a faint floral scent intermingled with the distinct fragrance of damp earth.

Vendrick had mentioned that the castle where Malachi had kidnapped and held me was once a residence of the previous King, abandoned when he favored the construction of this new palace. Still, I hadn't been prepared for the scale of this place. It was as if I had stepped into another realm; I had, yes, but this was unlike anything I'd encountered thus far.

With a hand on the small of my back, Vendrick guided me into the palace. My steps echoed along a corridor adorned with torches that cast flickering shadows upon the walls. The architecture was a symphony of gothic elegance, combining arches and vaulted ceilings with meticulously crafted stonework. The air was tinged with a chilliness that seemed to seep from the very stones.

Amidst the shadows, I caught glimpses of the guards patrolling the hallways. Each wore a cloak that seemed to meld seamlessly with the darkness. They were clad in armor that gleamed with an ebony sheen and were adorned with intricate engravings that seemed to shift and change as they moved.

Vendrick stood silently by my side, a patient smile on his lips. It was as if he knew the maelstrom of emotions clouding my thoughts, his presence a grounding force.

Before long, a guard approached us, the same Guard Captain who had delivered the King's summons after our battle against Malachi. Without a word, he motioned for us to follow him.

There were more intricate carvings adorning the corridor walls. They depicted scenes of battles, and moments of triumph. It was a visual history of the realm.

Finally, we were led into the throne room. King Aldric sat upon a throne seemingly hewn from the very heart of the earth. The stone was as black as the night sky, and its edges gleamed with an almost dangerous brilliance.

And it was floating.

The King himself was nothing like I had expected. I'd thought he would be old and pudgy, a stereotypical old rich man. But he defied those preconceptions entirely. He appeared to be in his sixties, though I had learned that age held a different meaning in this realm. His eyes were the same ethereal gold as Vendrick's, except they bore none of the same warmth. His long hair cascaded around him, but unlike Vendrick's dark locks, his were a shimmering shade of blond with flecks of silver. On top of his head was a slim gold band woven around emerald stones. He contrasted starkly against the darkness of the throne upon which he sat.

The throne room was an embodiment of grandeur and darkness, an intricate tapestry woven from obsidian stone and the glimmer of gold accents. The walls seemed to absorb the light, the shadows dancing with secrets and echoes of history. The Guard Captain, a stoic figure, stood at the foot of the throne, his cloak seamlessly blending into the shadowed corners of the room. His presence was the picture of loyalty and discipline, a guardian of the King's authority.

"You have summoned us, Your Majesty," Vendrick's voice broke the silence, his tone taking on an air of formality that was unfamiliar to me. It was as if he had donned a mask, concealing the layers of emotion and vulnerability I had come to recognize in him.

King Aldric's response was deliberate, allowing the tension to settle before he spoke. His voice resonated with authority, each word carrying weight. "Wayward son. I have had enough of your insolence. I have tolerated your disobedience thus far. But you have lied to your King and betrayed your oath."

The Guard Captain stepped forward, swiftly relieving Vendrick of his emerald sword. The weapon, which had seen us through countless challenges, now hung in the air like a testament to our vulnerability in this Court.

"You will be punished appropriately at dawn." The King's proclamation hung heavy in the air, like a storm cloud ready to break.

Then, the words could no longer be contained within me. "Your Majesty, your kingdom is falling apart," my voice cut through the chamber, each syllable imbued with determination. I stood taller, squaring my shoulders, meeting the King's gaze without hesitation.

As I reached over and took Vendrick's hand in mine, I felt a surge of conviction. He was my mate, and I was the Chosen One. My grip on his hand tightened, a gesture of solidarity and support.

"You do not interrupt His Majesty." The Guard Captain's voice was sharp and commanding, and he raised his gauntleted fist to hit me.

Vendrick caught hold of the Guard Captain's wrist, intercepting the strike.

"Lay a hand on my mate, Gerald, and I will break every bone in your body." His words carried the weight of a promise, each syllable laced with fierce protectiveness.

Vendrick summoned his shadows now, his eyes darting around as though he had given up on finding a civil end to this meeting, his mind perhaps already working out a strategy for escape.

"Enough!" King Aldric's voice boomed, reverberating through the grand chamber. The echoes of his command shattered any illusions of negotiation. "The Chosen One will be my guest. Send my son to the dungeons. He will face punishment at dawn."

Vendrick's posture visibly relaxed, a palpable relief washing over him as he registered that I would remain unharmed. His shadows dissipated as quickly as they had formed. However, my heart clenched with apprehension, my fingers instinctively reaching for his hand, seeking to lend him the strength of my support. But he withdrew his hand from mine, his decision clear. Surrender was his choice at this moment, as the guards began to lead him away, down a path that promised punishment and isolation.

"Chosen One, we will speak again at supper," the King's decree hung in the air, a promise or a warning.

I wanted to shout; I wanted to demand respect for Vendrick, to assert the bond we shared. But the King's subtle gesture, a flick of his wrist, set the Guard Captain, Gerald, into motion. With gentle yet firm guidance, he led me away from the throne room.

As I cast a final glance over my shoulder, Vendrick's figure grew smaller, his defiance and strength evident as he disappeared from view. I would have dinner with the King. I had to find a way to ensure that Vendrick was safe.

I paced restlessly within the confines of the spacious room where Gerald had unceremoniously left me. The room was beautiful, and the furnishings and decor exuded luxury. Yet, no amount of lavish surroundings could mask the unease that churned within me.

A small group of women had come in as Gerald left, their faces impassive as they went about their task, which was to prepare me for dinner with the King. Buckets of hot water were brought in, steam curling upward, filling the space with soothing warmth. Deft hands scrubbed my skin, fragrant soap leaving a pleasant aroma.

Once I was cleansed, they dressed me in a gown unlike anything I had ever seen. The fabric flowed like liquid obsidian, shimmering in the light, and it was adorned with intricate silver embroidery that caught every flicker of the torchlight. The dress clung to my form in all the right places before cascading into a sweeping train that trailed behind me as I moved.

Despite my badgering, the women maintained an unwavering silence throughout. My questions fell on deaf ears. When they were finished, they left as they had come. I guessed I was to await my summons alone then. Thoughts on how to save Vendrick from whatever the King had planned for dawn plagued my mind. I had to present a strong front.

Suddenly, the door burst open once more. One of the young women from before had returned, her head bowed slightly.

"His Majesty will see you now."

CHAPTER 14

VENDRICK

I 'm going to lose my mind in here.

My fingers traced the etchings on the stone walls of the cell I had been unceremoniously dumped into. The rough marks left by countless prisoners who had come before me told a story of resistance, desperation, and an unyielding spirit. Those walls had witnessed both rebellion and submission, defiance and despair. Now, they were bearing witness to my own predicament.

These cells were usually bustling with offenders, villagers thrown in for various offenses against royals, or those who'd fallen short of fulfilling their tax quotas. But today, they were empty—a stark testament to the recent winter solstice celebrations, during which many prisoners had faced the King's brutal justice.

The heavy silence wrapped around me like a shroud, punctuated only by the distant echoes of footsteps and hushed conversations drifting through the corridors. I'd always found solace in the shadows; their presence felt like a comforting embrace. But today, they felt like enemies, conspiring to keep me from the one thing I desired more than anything else—Ava, my mate, the light that banished all my inner darkness.

Leaning against the cool stone wall, my thoughts drifted to my escape. These walls couldn't truly contain me; I could slip through the shadows and disappear at will. My father knew this too well. The real leverage he held over me was the knowledge that he had *her*—Ava. He had heard the moment I'd acknowledged her as my mate. That bond superseded everything else in my life. He was counting on my determination to protect her to keep me in check.

I shuddered as my mind drifted back to Ava's defiance. My father was not known for his forgiveness or patience, yet she had stood against him— twice. And she was still around to tell the tale. Her boldness both worried and amazed me.

I was sure she hadn't grasped the full weight of her actions and how dangerously close she had come to losing her life.

My fingers itched for Skjor. I had never been apart from it since the day my father bestowed it on me.

I had stood at the base of the dais, uncertainty gnawing at me. The grand hall had always been a place of discomfort growing up, as I had rarely been allowed within its opulent walls, being a bastard son.

As a living testament to a liaison the King had wished to forget, I never dared to dream of inheriting the throne, nor did I yearn for it. Around the palace, they ensured I was aware of my status, never hesitating to remind me that I was inferior to other royals.

Then, against all odds, I came into my powers, and they came through stronger and wilder than anyone had predicted. That should have been the turning point, and it should have earned me recognition, respect, and a place of honor. Instead, my father continued to ignore me, dispatching me to the military to be trained under the Grand

Marshal. Before this time, everyone had thought I would be in the King's Guard. Mikal, the previous Guard Captain, had taken a liking to me from a young age, and thinking I had a future working with him had been a source of solace. That had been taken away from me.

But today, the King had summoned me. I had done well in the army; I had excelled in the last battle against the Light Court, playing a vital role in establishing the uneasy truce that now existed between both Courts as we searched for a solution to the ever-expanding Twisted Forest. I had done nothing wrong. Yet I was uneasy as I awaited the King's declaration.

"It is said that a kingdom is only as strong as its ruler's commitment to protect and serve his people," King Aldric began. Of course, he was going to be dramatic.

The courtiers whispered among themselves, curiosity and speculation swirling.

My gaze remained fixed on the pedestal beside him, where a sheathed sword rested, an emblem of power. The sheath was black as night, a void that swallowed all the light around it. The hilt, adorned with a resplendent emerald gem, caught my attention. It shimmered with an ethereal glow, starkly contrasting with the darkness that encased it. Skjor, they called it—Slayer. It was passed down from generation to generation and finally to my father. But it wasn't just a historical relic. It had been imbued with starlight by the first gods. It had the power to break through and destroy any spell of magic, including the curse within the Twisted Ones.

As King Aldric's voice droned on, my attention drifted. His words were grand, a mixture of self-praise and elaborate claims about the prosperity and order he had brought to the kingdom. I'd heard these speeches, always elaborate proclamations about his benevolent rule.

Eventually, he delved into the matter at hand. Honors and awards were being bestowed upon the nobles who had fought in the Last Battle against the forces of the Light Court. His voice faded into the background until a name pulled me back to the present—my name.

"...and to my son, Vendrick," the words reverberated through the hall, sending a jolt of surprise through me. He was acknowledging my existence, my role in the battle, something he had rarely done before. "For his exceptional valor and strategic acumen in the Last Battle, I name him First Field Marshal of the Royal Army."

My heart raced, each beat echoing the shock and disbelief that surged through me. Slowly, deliberately, I made my way to the dais, each step feeling like an eternity. The eyes of the Court were upon me, a mixture of surprise and curiosity in their gazes. The weight of their attention was almost palpable, a physical pressure that bore down on me.

I reached the dais, my movements mechanical as I extended my arm to receive the King's pin. As I stepped back, the pin gleaming on my chest, the King motioned that I remain. He reached for Skjor, the sword that lay upon the pedestal beside him.

My heart skipped a beat, uncertainty flooding my senses. What was he doing? I turned to face him, and his outstretched arm held the sword toward me. My breath caught in my throat, my heart pounding louder in my ears.

I hesitated for a moment before sinking to one knee. My head bowed, and I extended my hands to receive the sword. The hilt met my open palms, and for a moment, time seemed to stand still, a shiver running down my spine like a current of energy had passed through me.

As I pulled the sword to myself, I felt its magic resonate with my own. It was as if Skjor recognized me as if it had been waiting for this connection. The hilt seemed to warm under my touch, and as I slowly drew the sword from its sheath, a brilliant blade shone forth.

I rose to my feet, the sword held before me, its brilliance casting a glow upon my face. I met my father's gaze, a rare moment of connection passing between us. The questions and uncertainties would come later, I knew. But for now, I was content to face whatever consequences lay ahead.

* * *

I had paid the price. After my first mission as Field Marshal, I returned to a forever-altered kingdom. Mikal, my childhood friend and confidant, was dead. In his place, his first son Gerald had ascended to the role of Guard Captain. The dynamics had shifted, and allegiances had been solidified.

All appeals for urgent aid to the villagers who lived on the edge of the Twisted Forest, where the Twisted Ones roamed, were met with indifference. The pleas were ignored, and it became evident that the lives hanging in the balance were of little concern to those who held authority. I stood as the lone shield between the vulnerable people and the encroaching darkness.

A sudden commotion echoed through the prison corridors, jolting me out of my thoughts. The usual stillness of the cells was shattered by the urgent footsteps of guards rushing in every direction. Instinctively, I hurried to the bars of my cell, gripping them tightly as I strained to catch snippets of conversation.

My heart raced, a mixture of anxiety and curiosity tightening my chest. What could have disrupted the usual routine of the palace to this extent? My mind immediately flickered to Ava. Was she safe? Muffled words and urgent tones only added to my growing unease.

Ava's safety was my priority, and realizing that I couldn't guarantee it from this cell prompted me to step into the shadows and out of it.

CHAPTER 15

AVA

As the young woman— Cyla— guided me to dinner, she shared that this was the King's private dining chamber. For someone who'd probably been asked to remain silent, she sure chatted a lot. But her chattering brought a smile to my face. She was the only other friendly face that had come my way since I came to the Dark Realm.

Lucien, the Guard Captain's second, joined me when my attendant left me. After introducing himself, he began to interpret what was the prophecy about the Chosen One, etched in an ancient language among vibrant murals adorning the secluded dining chamber.

In the dark days, when corruption creeps and lingers.

And the shadows and light diverge,

She comes forth,

Of both realms birthed, two spirits aligned,

To mend, shatter, and banish,

Confronting the darkness till the battle is won,

A saga echoing long after it's finished.

Questions lingered in my mind. How had they discerned my role as the one in this cryptic verse? The prophecy's vagueness gnawed at my thoughts. Could their assumption be incorrect?

I banished such doubts; they held no value in this moment. My focus remained on Vendrick, my heart yearning for him. The brief time we'd spent apart now felt like an eternity.

Servants flowed in with a bounty of dishes. I had never seen so much food in one place in all my life.

Without warning, Lucien shifted his attention from the prophecy to the door, standing at full attention. The atmosphere shifted as the King entered, casting an imposing presence over the room.

Steeling myself, I strode purposefully toward the grand table, summoning every ounce of decorum I could muster. This encounter needed to unfold flawlessly; the stakes were beyond anything I had encountered before — my mate's life.

"Your Majesty, I am deeply grateful for your gracious invitation," I ventured, offering a slight bow as my fingers toyed nervously with the edge of my gown.

With practiced ease, King Aldric ignored my pleasantries and claimed his seat at the table. I followed suit, my movements slightly hesitant, guided by the servants' orchestrated gestures. Lucien and the accompanying guards remained stoically by the walls.

As the ornate silver food domes were lifted, revealing a tantalizing array of dishes, a pleasant aroma filled the atmosphere. But my nerves prevented me from enjoying any of it.

"You are mated to my bastard," the King stated rather than asking as he appraised me.

His assertion about my connection to Vendrick jolted me, his slur raising my hackles. I reminded myself that diplomacy and restraint were my allies here.

I picked at the unfamiliar food, never really putting anything in my mouth. I knew they had food like I had back in the human realm, but nothing here was familiar, trying to disorient me.

"Yes," I answered, even though the King had not asked.

"I have a proposition for you," he said, accepting the wine another servant held out to him. I dropped the facade of eating, picking up a glass of water, anticipating what he was about to propose.

"My brother thinks to overthrow me."

I froze, the glass of water halfway to my lips. Of course, the King knew about Malachi, but what was he about to propose?

A sudden crash from an adjoining room interrupted King Aldric's proposition. The adjoining room's door crashed open with a force that echoed through the chamber, and all eyes swiveled toward the commotion.

Gerald, the Guard Captain, rushed in urgently, reaching for King Aldric's wine goblet and sending it crashing on the other side of the room.

A hushed exchange passed between them, too soft for my ears to catch, yet the grim tension on King Aldric's face revealed the gravity of their conversation. With Gerald's whispered words, the mood shifted from tense anticipation to palpable alarm.

A heavy silence settled in, punctuated only by the distant sounds of muttering and horrible coughs emanating from the adjacent room.

We all waited, straining to decipher anything about what was going on there. Then, a resounding thud reverberated in the silence.

Pandemonium ensued.

Lucien swiftly escorted me out of the dining room and back to the room that had been designated for me. His tone was low, his words laced with a seriousness that sent shivers down my spine. "Bolt the door behind me," he instructed, his gaze intense as he ensured I followed his command. I slid the bolt into place, the sound resonating like a final barrier against the unknown.

I was left alone in the room, the weight of confusion and apprehension settling on my shoulders. Something had gone terribly wrong, but I was left in the dark again. All I could think about was Vendrick, the man who had become my anchor in this unfamiliar world—the one who made me feel like I finally belonged, like I had found my rightful place.

My thoughts reached out to him, a silent plea that echoed in my mind. *Vendrick, wherever you are, whatever is happening, I wish you were with me. Let's face whatever comes together.*

Time felt distorted as I waited, my anxiety mounting with each passing moment.

Lucien returned swiftly, but his composed demeanor had given way to urgency. Outside the room, the corridor was alive with a chaotic dance of guards. Their hurried movements and tense expressions spoke volumes. My heart raced, a mixture of fear and anticipation gripping me.

Lucien's urgency was palpable, his actions communicating a need for swift action. I moved forward, prepared to confront whatever awaited us beyond the door.

"What's happening?" I demanded, my anxiety mounting with every passing second.

"Come with me," he replied urgently, guiding me in the direction opposite the tumultuous commotion where guards were hastening.

"Malachi has attacked the palace with a horde of Twisted Ones." Lucien's words hit me like a shockwave, leaving me momentarily stunned.

"Malachi has gained control over them."

My mind raced to process this horrifying revelation. Malachi's name sent shivers down my spine, and the mention of Twisted Ones filled me with dread.

"Vendrick!" The word burst from my lips, a mixture of fear and desperation coloring my voice. "We need to find Vendrick, now," I implored Lucien, my heart driving me to action. I turned, ready to head in a direction, any direction that might lead me to Vendrick's side.

I'm coming to you, Starlight, I'm coming. I heard Vendrick's response as it floated down the mate-bond.

Turning a corner, we abruptly found ourselves in the midst of a tense battle. Lucien quickly pivoted, leading me in another direction as the clash of metal and guttural roars filled the air. But there was no escape — more Twisted Ones materialized from the shadows, blocking our path.

Lucien shielded me, placing himself between me and the impending threat. His determination to defend me was clear, yet I had grown tired of being shielded. I was no longer the powerless human stumbling into a hidden world. I was the Chosen One, a force to be reckoned with, and I held the power to shape my own destiny.

I tossed a ball of light at one of the Twisted Ones coming for Lucien, and it shrieked as it shriveled up into dust.

He turned in amazement to just stare at me. I just shrugged at him, and with little effort, I conjured Dawnbreaker. The sword manifested in a blaze of light. Since the mate-bond settled in place, I could manipulate my light more easily.

I ripped off the train of the beautiful dress I was wearing. It was the only way I could fight. Another flicker of surprise crossed Lucien's eyes, his expression shifting from protector to partner as he positioned himself back-to-back with me.

Together, we charged into the midst of the horde.

CHAPTER 16

VENDRICK

Vendrick!

The urgency in Ava's voice reverberated through the mate-bond, igniting a surge of adrenaline through my veins. Every fiber of my being compelled me to reach her side, to ensure her safety in the chaos that was unfolding. I quickened my pace. *I'm coming to you, Starlight, I'm coming!*

I maneuvered through the palace's corridors, pushing past guards who were rushing in every direction. None of them questioned my presence or what I was doing outside my cell—the impending threat seemed to have rendered normal protocol irrelevant. One young soldier, his eyes wide with a mix of fear and confusion, halted as I jerked him to a stop.

"What's happening?" I demanded, my tone urgent.

"Malachi...Twisted Ones," he stammered, his voice shaky. It was evident that he was inexperienced in battle, his fear palpable. In a different circumstance, I might have taken him under my wing, ensuring his protection and guiding him through the chaos. But at that moment, my only priority was Ava's safety.

"What's your name, soldier?" I asked urgently, shaking him in an attempt to snap him back to alertness.

"Dylan, Sir," he responded, blinking as he gathered his bearings.

"Dylan, head to the south wall and inform them that the First Field Marshal commands them to alert the Sixth Garrison," I instructed swiftly.

The Sixth Garrison was under my command, stationed at Blackwood. Its captain, a friend of mine, would know how to respond to the situation. Sending Dylan to the south wall would also get him away from the immediate battlefront, which was my priority as the Twisted Ones seemed to be attacking from the west wing.

If Malachi had indeed infiltrated the palace, then he would be looking for Ava, so I needed to find her before he did. I took a moment to focus on our mate-bond. It had been feeding me snippets of information from her, assuring me that she was alive and not critically hurt. But I needed to find her, to hold her, and assure myself that she was okay. I closed my eyes, letting the unique resonance of our bond guide me. A vivid image of her holding Dawnbreaker, her light sword, materialized in my mind's eye.

I reached for Dylan's sword at his side—he hadn't even drawn it. Placing it in his hand, I sent him on his way with a swift nudge.

Drawing a deep breath, I summoned my shadows, letting them envelop me and transport me to where Ava was. Time was of the essence.

"Heads up!"

That was my only warning as something came flying at me as soon as I materialized out of the shadows—Skjor. Lucien had thrown it. And Lucien was fighting near Ava, protecting her. No way to escape it; I was in Lucien's debt now.

Lucien and I had grown up in the Dark Court together. His mother was a cousin of my father's, and his father had infamously eloped with a princess from the Light Court, leaving a trail of scandal behind him. Lucien had always treated me amicably despite my status as a royal bastard.

I nodded my gratitude in his direction.

"It's about time you joined us," the other half of my soul said as she barreled into me, holding me tight, her relief palpable. She scrutinized me for any signs of injury before her gaze softened. "Are you hurt?"

A shield of pure light materialized around us as I pulled her in to kiss her deeply.

"I'm alright, Starlight. Now that I've found you, everything is alright," I whispered, overwhelmed by the surge of relief that coursed through me. We were united, and together, we could face whatever challenges lay ahead.

As Ava let the light shield fall, she threw Dawnbreaker at a Twisted One that had been sneaking up behind Lucien, which collapsed with a moan on the floor.

She allowed the sword to disappear and reform in her hands. She was stronger than she'd ever been.

We threw ourselves back into the fray. Ava's protective shield enveloped us again, and side by side, we fought against the advancing horde of Twisted Ones. Our blades cleaved through the creatures. We swung and hacked away at them until, before long, there were none standing.

But some writhed on the ground, not turning into dust as they typically did. This was different.

Lucien and I exchanged a glance, our shared confusion apparent. We began to step forward, ready to deliver the final blow to the suffering creatures when Ava's voice cut through.

"Wait!" she called, a mix of caution and curiosity in her tone. "Look at them, Vendrick. Look."

Intrigued, I approached one of the fallen Twisted Ones, studying it closely.

Dark tendrils of smoke flowed from the twisted forms, and a revelation dawned upon me—they were reverting to their former state. Shadowkin. The very creatures that had been consumed by darkness were becoming Shadowkin once more.

"Chosen One," Lucien's voice was a reverent whisper, his gesture a deep bow of respect to Ava.

Dawnbreaker, it seemed, held a power beyond our understanding, a power to cleanse the darkness and reclaim lost souls. A surge of awe and pride swelled within me, and I pulled Ava close.

As our moment of astonishment waned, her voice cut through, her focus unwavering. "We need to find the King. I'm certain that's where Malachi is heading."

Lucien nodded, his expression grave. "He was poisoned during dinner."

Ava was right. Though my relationship with my father was strained at best, Malachi was the greater threat by far.

But even as the urgency of the situation pressed upon us, I couldn't help but marvel at Ava's power. She was the key to defeating the Twisted Ones and redeeming those lost to darkness. Dawnbreaker had proven itself a weapon of hope.

"For now, we must focus on stopping Malachi," I agreed, my voice steady despite the chaos around us. "Once he's dealt with, we can aid these Shadowkin. They deserve a chance to reclaim their lives."

Ava nodded, her eyes shining with resolve.

The frantic echoes of battle reverberated through the palace's corridors. But it was evident that the tide had started to shift in our favor, the reinforcements of the Sixth Garrison making a crucial impact on the battle's outcome. But we couldn't afford to be complacent. We raced toward the King's chambers.

Upon breaching the outer chamber, the scene was one of turmoil and desperation. The King's Guard were being overrun. Without hesitation, Lucien and I dove into the fray, our intention clear—to incapacitate rather than kill. Each strike by the light sword left tendrils of darkness pouring through the wound as Ava and Dawnbreaker strived to save as many as they could of those whom the Twisted Ones' curse had ensnared.

Moving through the chambers, we found Gerald. The Captain was the last guard standing against the onslaught. His weary eyes met mine, and I could see the determination burning within him. Lucien joined him immediately.

Malachi remained elusive, but our primary concern was the King's safety.

"How is the King?" I inquired urgently, my heart pounding with a mixture of apprehension and dread.

"The palace physicians are attending to him," Gerald answered, his voice grim. "They believe it's Ormkyss root poisoning."

The mention of Ormkyss root struck me like a blow. It was a rare and deadly poison; it could only be found in the heart of the Twisted Forest.

Malachi. This was Malachi's doing. The realization hit me like a punch in the gut.

"Get me to him. Maybe I can heal him," Ava spoke up.

Her suggestion made sense; her healing abilities were unparalleled, having proven time and again her capacity to mend even the deepest wounds. My heart swelled with admiration for her strength, but I couldn't help but notice the toll the day's events had taken on her. Her energy seemed depleted. Though Dawnbreaker remained vibrant in her hand, her fireballs flickered into mere sparks.

I nodded in agreement, acknowledging her proposal. We needed to act swiftly; her intervention might be our last hope to save the King. Gerald was in no place to argue. He simply turned and led us forward.

Finally reaching the King's bedchamber, we were met with the grim scene of the palace physicians tending to my father. He was slumped in bed, his usually robust behavior was now diminished, his skin pallid and his breathing shallow.

Ava wasted no time as she approached the King's bedside. "Let me try."

CHAPTER 17

AVA

T he King looked like death. The color had seeped out of him. His brilliant gold eyes were now gray and sightless. I didn't know what to do, but knew I had to do something.

The palace physicians had not budged at my plea to let me attempt my healing spell.

"Everybody, step back!" Gerald barked.

His authoritative tone spurred the physicians into reluctant compliance. They moved away, their expressions a mixture of skepticism and resignation. They knew that there was little they could do.

I stepped toward the King with a deep breath and extended my hands over him. The air in the room grew tense as my powers enveloped him. I could feel the weight of his ailment, a darkness that seemed to resist my efforts. My hands trembled slightly as I concentrated, my heart pounding in my chest.

For a moment, it felt like time had frozen. The room was hushed, every gaze fixed on me and the ailing King. My mind was a whirlwind of determination and doubt. Could I truly heal him?

It would not be enough. I just knew it.

A surge of fatigue washed over me, threatening to pull me under. I could feel the strain on my reserves, my body protesting the immense effort. The light around the King wavered, flickering like a candle in the wind. Desperation clawed at the edges of my mind. The room spun around me, and just as I felt my legs give way, I was caught by strong arms.

Vendrick.

"You're not alone in this," he murmured against my ear, his breath a reassuring whisper.

I felt a wave of energy, Vendrick's energy beginning to flow into me through our mate-bond. I was surprised.

"How?" I asked.

"I don't know how, but we have to make the most of it right now," Vendrick replied, his voice full of wonder and urgency.

With this unexpected infusion of power, I steadied myself and focused once again on the King. The light that emanated from me was no longer just mine; it shimmered with the intertwining dance of light and shadow. It was as if our bond had amplified not only our connection but also our abilities.

As the combined energy enveloped King Aldric, I sensed a subtle shift. It was as if this new amalgamation of power had found a way to penetrate the depths of his ailment. Slowly, the color began to return to his ashen features, and a glimmer of hope flickered in my heart.

But the truth could not be denied: time was running out. The poison had ravaged him too deeply, and the battle to save him was far from over. I couldn't shake the feeling that we were racing against a merciless clock.

"You truly are the Chosen One." King Aldric's voice was weak, but his gaze held a mixture of admiration and gratitude. He motioned for me to come closer, and I obeyed, leaning in to hear his words.

"I knew your father," he continued, his voice carrying the weight of memories long buried. "He had been a dear friend of mine until he fell in love with that princess they sent as an emissary from the Light Court."

His words struck me like a bolt of lightning. My parents had been nothing more than distant shadows in my mind, their faces shrouded in mystery. The only thing I knew about them was that they had died when I was young. Since I'd come to the Shadow Realm, I knew they couldn't have been human but Shadowkin. At least one of them had to be for me to have the powers I did. But this, I had not expected this.

The revelation that my father had been part of this world, that he'd known the King, that he'd fallen in love with a princess from the Light Court was all too much to process.

I had so many questions and asked them all. What happened to my parents? Why did they have to flee to the human world? How did they die? What did it all have to do with me becoming the Chosen One?

The King hurried now; he knew his time was short.

He answered as many questions as he could. My parents' relationship was forbidden in both Courts, so to escape the fury of the Light Queen and the Dark King, they fled to the human realm, even though they could have been the cause of a peace treaty. My father had been Dark Shadowkin royalty, and my mother had been the strongest light healer across the entire realm.

I had a half-brother—Lucien.

No one had answers about how they died. There was no other reason to point to my being the Chosen One except that my parents were from both Courts.

The King's breathing grew shallower, his strength waning. He had shared what he could, a piece of the puzzle that had been concealed for so long. I wanted to press for more answers, but time was mercilessly slipping through our fingers.

Vendrick's arm was the only thing still holding me up. The King was going to die. That much was obvious now. I stepped back so that Gerald could receive his final words.

"Get me out of here, *please*," I said.

CHAPTER 18

VENDRICK

I gently stroked Ava's arm, trying to provide some semblance of comfort amidst the chaos that surrounded us. The weight of the King's revelation still hung heavy in the air, a tangled web of emotions that we both needed to unravel. My attempt to reach out through our mate-bond was met with a wall, leaving me with more questions than answers.

"Go and say your goodbyes to your father, Vendrick. We need to find Malachi," Ava's voice cut through my thoughts.

I didn't understand what sort of strength she had. Her ability to focus on the task at hand, even amidst the turmoil, was nothing short of remarkable. But there was nowhere else I'd rather be than at her side. Protecting her, even though she could defend herself.

Also, I felt resistance at the prospect of bidding my father farewell. My relationship with the King had been strained at best, marred by years of resentment and neglect. What more was there to say?

"I have nothing more to say to the King," I replied, my voice a mixture of frustration and exhaustion.

Ava's eyes bore into mine, her expression torn between understanding and insistence. Before she could respond, a guttural growl reverberated through the antechamber, its intensity sending a shiver down my spine.

Ava and I exchanged a quick glance, our instincts instantly on high alert. This was not a sound that belonged to the realm of men or Shadowkin. It was something primal, something unnatural.

My hand instinctively went to the hilt of Skjor as I turned toward the source of the growl.

Lucien burst through the door, struggling to catch his breath.

"We have more company," Lucien's voice was calm, but the urgency beneath it was unmistakable. "And more Twisted Ones."

Another roar echoed through the chamber as a Twisted One unlike any we had faced before materialized right behind Lucien. It had humanoid height and build, but its eyes now resembled blackened coals, devoid of humanity. Its figure was contorted into an unsettling grotesque shape, a reflection of the darkness that now consumed it.

"You ungrateful wench," it spat, "I would have given you the world!"

"Malachi?" Ava inquired.

A wicked chuckle rumbled from the creature's throat.

"Seeing what a monster you've become, I'm really glad I turned down your offer," she retorted. Her voice was laced with disgust and a touch of contempt.

The insult seemed to strike a nerve, and in an instant, Malachi lunged. His twisted form moved with unnatural speed, his hand reaching out to seize Ava. With a sickening thud, he smashed her to the ground, her body crumpling under the force of the impact.

The sight of her attacked ignited a fury within me that burned hotter than anything I'd ever experienced. "Ava!" The name tore from my lips as I checked the bond to see how hurt she was. When I confirmed that she was fine, I launched myself at Malachi. Every ounce of my strength, every drop of my determination, was channeled into that single act.

There were others with him, and they flooded the room. They seemed sentient, just like Lucien had stated. The guards and soldiers went to work, fighting them while Ava and I focused on Malachi.

CHAPTER 19

AVA

M^{erge.} Dawnbreaker was whispering to me, a faint call echoing in my mind. It seemed to yearn for a union, a merging, yet its intentions remained cryptic. Despite the urgency of the battle, I couldn't shake the sensation that the sword held a secret I needed to unlock. Malachi's unnatural speed blurred the fight, making it challenging to keep up. Vendrick was hanging on, but the odds were against us. A miracle was our only hope now.

Merge!

Dawnbreaker's fervent whisper surged once more, and a stream of light flowed from it toward Vendrick. *Merge with him?* I questioned through our mind link. Strangely, Dawnbreaker emanated an aura almost haughty in its insistence. Fine. If it didn't want to merge with Vendrick, then what did it seek? The light swirled again insistently in that direction.

I watched as Vendrick swung Skjor at Malachi, only for Malachi to knock the sword away. The weapon skidded to a halt at my feet, and in that moment, Dawnbreaker's light shifted direction once more.

A realization dawned upon me—it wanted to merge with Vendrick's sword.

I didn't hesitate. Bending down, I picked up Skjor, feeling the resonance of its power coursing through my grip.

As Dawnbreaker dissolved from my grip, it flowed like ethereal mist into the Skjor. The moment it made contact, a brilliant radiance burst forth, illuminating the entire room in a blinding cascade of light.

CHAPTER 20

VENDRICK

B linding light filled the room, but I was not surprised; I knew exactly what was happening. Our mate-bond transformed in a new way. Skjor—I had never felt like the name fit my emerald sword until that moment. After the swords merged, it grew to twice its size, and blinding light poured from all angles.

Slayer.

Ava seemed to grow as well, becoming ensconced in light. She wielded Skjor like it was made for her.

Malachi turned toward the new threat, hesitant now, yet still determined. With a long guttural growl, he lunged at her one last time.

Her sword flowed cleanly through him, his twisted form disintegrating as if it was nothing more than mist touched by dawn's first light. A wail of anguish filled the air as he faded into oblivion.

The remaining Twisted Ones shrieked and howled, their forms crumbling away in the presence of the merged swords' radiance. It was as if their twisted existence couldn't withstand the purity of the light.

Ava stood at the center of the room, radiant like a goddess of old. This was the true Chosen One.

There was a certain detachment in her expression, a distant look that was completely unlike her usual warmth and determination.

As the soldiers celebrated around her, I stepped closer, my heart pounding with a mix of awe and concern. The power radiating from her was undeniable, but it felt different somehow, tinged with an otherworldly energy that I couldn't quite grasp.

"Ava?" I murmured, reaching out a hand to her. She turned her gaze toward me, and for a moment, I saw a glimmer of recognition in her eyes. But it was quickly replaced by that distant, unyielding look.

Her voice resonated, carrying an eerie echo. "I am the embodiment of light and shadow, the balance that must be restored."

This was not my mate.

CHAPTER 21

AVA

I was drowning.

Dawnbreaker had taken over my mind and I no longer had control. And she was angry. She wanted more destruction, but Skjorhad destroyed all the remaining Twisted Ones just with its radiance.

"Tainted. Evil has taken over this realm, and it must be cleansed," Dawnbreaker said through my mouth. It didn't sound like a bad thing, but I knew what she meant. She meant to destroy all life in the Dark Court. I could not allow that. These people had suffered enough under King Aldric and Malachi. This was supposed to be their chance at a new life. I would not let this ancient goddess destroy them just because she didn't understand that good and evil coexist for balance to occur.

I had to fight, but I had no strength left. It felt so good to let go of my control, let someone else be in charge for a change.

Starlight, Vendrick's voice came through our mate-bond. *My strong warrior. Fight a little longer for me.*

I reached out, trying to hold on to him, but he seemed too far away, and I was so tired. I wanted to rest, just a little. Just a little.

CHAPTER 22

VENDRICK

"Ava!"

The cry tore from me through our mate-bond, desperation clawing at my chest as I sensed her presence slipping away, fading into an unsettling gray void.

"Return her to me!" I yelled at the figure that looked like Ava but was not. "I beg you, return the one I love. I'll do whatever it takes."

My voice was ragged, the pain in my heart palpable. I fell to my knees, unable to bear the weight of the moment. Tears streamed down my face as I clutched my chest, as if I could physically hold onto the bond that was slipping through my fingers.

Suddenly, Lucien was by my side, his strong presence a grounding force. He placed a hand on my shoulder, offering silent support as my world seemed to crumble around me.

"Remember how you channeled your energy into Ava when she tried to heal the King?" Lucien's voice was a lifeline amidst the chaos. "Try it again now. Your connection might be the key to saving her."

I drew upon the mate-bond, the wellspring of emotions and shared experiences that bound us together. And with all the intensity of my heart, I pushed my energy through the bond, pouring it into her, into the very essence of what made her Ava.

For a brief moment, I felt a flicker of recognition. It was as if a door had opened, allowing a small glimpse of the person I loved to shine through. But then, the barrier seemed to solidify again, the void resuming its grip.

"She's in there," I whispered, tears mingling with my words.

CHAPTER 23

AVA

"Ava! I need you."

Vendrick. I couldn't leave him. He was my mate; he would be alone without me. I swore never to abandon him. I mustered all that was left in me and reached to him through the bond. I felt our essences reconnect, and I held on. His energy poured into me.

Leave. Dawnbreaker, your work here is done, I declared, pushing her out with our joint strength. Just like that, my body was my own again.

And I collapsed into Vendrick's arms for the second time that day.

CHAPTER 24

VENDRICK

A s the first rays of daybreak filtered through the remnants of the palace, a weary calm settled over the battlefield. The air was thick with the residue of magic and the aftermath of battle. Exhaustion hung heavy in the air, a palpable reminder of the trials throughout the night. The once-glorious palace now bore scars, its walls echoing with the clash of forces that had fought within its confines.

Amidst the wreckage, a sense of purpose emerged from the chaos.

But there was much to be done, and someone needed to step forward to lead. The King was dead. Malachi had fallen. The Shadowkin saved from their twisted fate were a testament of hope. As First Field Marshal, the mantle of responsibility had fallen upon my shoulders. It was time to rise to the occasion.

I put the Sixth Garrison in charge of the cleanup of the palace. The Royal Guard I put in charge of finding clothing for the rehabilitated Twisted Ones. They would be examined thoroughly tomorrow before we reunited them with their families and decided what to do with those who didn't have anyone.

After ensuring every duty was assigned, I made it clear that I was not to be disturbed for the next several hours. My body ached with fatigue; I headed toward my own quarters within the palace. There, amidst the soft flicker of candlelight, lay Ava. Her features were serene in sleep.

I slipped into the space beside her, drawing her into my embrace. The exhaustion that had been held at bay now surged forward, its grip unrelenting. But as I closed my eyes and held Ava close, the weight of my responsibilities, the tumult of the night, all faded into the background.

For now, there was only us in this fleeting moment of respite.

EPILOGUE

AVA

I slept for three days straight.

"Hello, half-sister." Lucien was by my bed when I woke up, panicking for Vendrick. "Hey, he's fine. I just sent him to get a shower. He would not leave your bedside the last three days."

You had me worried, Starlight. Vendrick's voice came loud and clear through the bond. *You don't want to know what I will do to you if you scare me like that again.*

Oh, we can do this now? I responded, the smile in my mental voice evident.

Lucien cleared his throat. "I don't know what's going on with you people, but I'm still here, your brother. I don't need to know what's making you smile like that."

Vendrick sauntered back into the room, coming to kiss me and tuck me back into his arms as Lucien gave us the report.

Malachi had brought all the Twisted Ones of the Forbidden Forest here, where they'd been destroyed or restored. We only needed to figure out what to do about the forest itself. The Light Court was sending an entourage with a company of Healers. We would figure out how to destroy the forest when they arrived. This would allow me to learn more about my other half and my mother. Who knew I could have more family in the Light Court. I was nervous and excited, but would not be alone this time.

Vendrick refused to become the new King, suggesting a civilian government run by the people, with equal representation from the commoners and royals. It was all a lot to process. And we would handle that all later.

"I'll make sure the two of you have the rest of the day without disturbance," Lucien said with a wink as he walked out of our chambers, leaving us in our cocoon of love and happiness.

I turned to admire Vendrick as he held me. His eyes were already on me, a suspicious grin playing on his lips. He pulled me up to him, burying his face in the crook of my neck. "There's a lot left to do." Vendrick's voice muffled as trailed kisses along my nape. I leaned into him, just enjoying the moment.

"Ready to rebuild, Starlight?" Vendrick asked as he came up for air.

"With you beside me, I am ready for anything," I replied, an answering smile on my face as I pulled him in for a kiss.

Made in the USA
Monee, IL
27 October 2023